Opposites:

Hard and Soft

Luana K. Mitten

Rourke

Publishing LLC
Vero Beach, Florida 32964

© 2009 Rourke Publishing LLC

www.rourkepublishing.com

PHOTO CREDITS: © oneclearvision: page 3 left; © Jose Manuel Gelpi Diaz: page 3 right; © Paul Tessier: page 5; © James Robinson: page 6, 7; © Marzanna Syncerz: page 9 right; © Tony Campbell: page 9 left; © Bulent Ince: page 10, 11; © Liza McCorkle: page 13 bottom; © Jarek Syzmanski: page 13 top; © Eileen Hart: page 14, 15; © William Murphey: page 17 top; © Craig Lopetz: page 17 bottom; © Robert Dant: page 18, 19; © Narvikk: page 21 bottom, 22; © Eric Isselée: page 21 top

Editor: Kelli Hicks

Cover design by Nicola Stratford, bdpublishing.com

Interior Design by Heather Botto

Library of Congress Cataloging-in-Publication Data

Mitten, Luana K.
  Opposites : hard and soft / Luana K. Mitten.
      p. cm. -- (Concepts)
  Learning the concept of opposites through riddles and poetry.
  ISBN 978-1-60472-419-6 (hardcover)
  ISBN 978-1-60472-815-6 (softcover)
  1. English language--Synonyms and antonyms--Juvenile literature. 2. Riddles, juvenile. I. Title.
  PE1591.M645 2008
  423'.1--dc22

                        2008018799

Printed in the USA

CG/CG

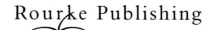

Rourke Publishing

www.rourkepublishing.com – rourke@rourkepublishing.com
Post Office Box 3328, Vero Beach, FL 32964

Hard and soft, soft and hard, what's the difference between hard and soft?

My bill is hard.

My feathers are soft.

What am I?

5

A duck

6

7

My claws are hard.

My fur is soft.

What am I?

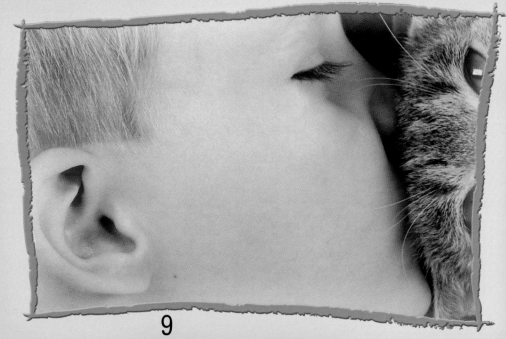

9

A cat

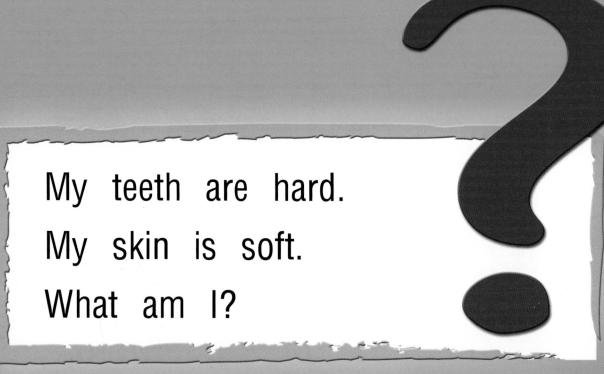

My teeth are hard.
My skin is soft.
What am I?

13

A person

15

My snout is hard.
My fur is soft.
What am I?

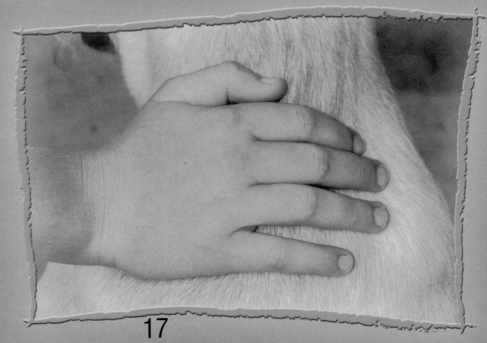

17

A   dog

19

My hooves are hard.

My tail is soft.

What am I?

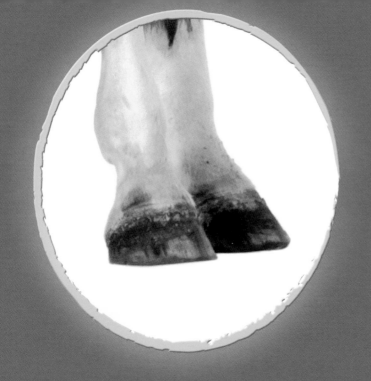

21

A horse

Hard and soft, soft and hard, now you know the difference between hard and soft.

Hard

Soft

23

Index

Further Reading

Child, Lauren. *Charlie and Lola's Opposites.* 2007.

Ford, Bernette. Sorrentino, Christiano. *A Big Dog: An Opposites Book,* 2008.

Falk, Laine. *Let's Talk About Opposites: Morning to Night,* 2007.

Holland, Gina. *Soft and Hard (I Know My Opposites),* 2007.

Recommended Websites

www.abcteach.com/grammar/online/opposites1.htm

www.resources.kaboose.com/games/read1html

www.learn4good.com/kids/preschool_english_spanish_language_books.htm

About the Author

Luana Mitten lives in Tampa, Florida. She likes walking on the soft, sandy beaches to collect hard seashells.